Excalibur
the
Magic Sword

Tony Mitton

Illustrated by Arthur Robins

ORCHARD BOOKS

CRAZY CAMELOT

MEET THE KNIGHTS OF THE ROUND TABLE:

King Arthur
with his sword so bright,

Sir Percival,
a wily knight.

Sir Kay,
a chap whose hopes are high,

Sir Lancelot,
makes ladies sigh.

Sir Gawain,
feeling rather green,

Sir Galahad,
so young and keen.

Sir Ack,
who's fond of eating lots,

Sir Mordred,
hatching horrid plots.

Morgana,
Arthur's wicked
sister,

Merlin.
That's me,
your wizard mister!

*To Sir Ralph of Bradmore Park,
valiant knight, from Tony Mitton,
Scribe to the Wizard Merlin*

*To Sir Hayden Thomas Skerry,
from Arthur Robins*

ORCHARD BOOKS
96 Leonard Street, London EC2A 4XD
Orchard Books Australia
32/45-51 Huntley Street, Alexandria, NSW 2015
First published in Great Britain in 2003
First paperback edition 2004
Text © Tony Mitton 2003
Illustrations © Arthur Robins 2003
The rights of Tony Mitton to be identified as the author
and Arthur Robins as the illustrator of this work
have been asserted by them in accordance with the
Copyright, Designs, and Patents Act, 1988.
A CIP catalogue record for this book is available
from the British Library.
ISBN 1 84121 716 6 (hardback)
ISBN 1 84121 718 2 (paperback)
1 3 5 7 9 10 8 6 4 2 (hardback)
1 3 5 7 9 10 8 6 4 2 (paperback)
Printed in Great Britain

Back in the Middle Ages,
brave knights wore suits of tin.
Whenever they changed their underwear
it made a monstrous din.

But though they were really noisy,
they were honest, kind and true.
And they clanked around until they found
exciting things to do.

The knights of Camelot had a table,
round and made of wood.
They sat there with King Arthur,
who was handsome, brave and good.

I am the wizard Merlin,
the royal magic-fella.
I know the tales of Camelot,
so I'm your story-teller.

Now, let me take a good old gulp
from my magic story cup.
And then let's spin the table
to see which tale pops up.

Aha, there's something coming now...
What will it be...? O-ho!
The tale of Great Excalibur,
the finest sword I know.

This story takes us back to when
King Arthur's court was new.
Although he'd got his kingship,
his followers were few.

Arthur was still a youngster,
a cheerful, jolly lad.
He loved to shout, and charge about,
and act a little mad.

The land was full of barons
who said, "It just ain't right
that this young clown should wear
the crown."

Sir Pellinore was one of these,
a nasty bully boy.
Defying kings and breaking things
brought Pellinore great joy.

He loved to ride across the land.
He loved to loot and pillage.
He loved to make the peasants quake
by swaggering round their village.

And news soon came to Arthur's ears
that Pellinore had said,
"This Arthur boy is just a toy.
I'll clout him round the head!"

Young Arthur heard these words
    and growled,
"That rough and rowdy knight!
I'll teach him not to talk like that.
I'll seal his lips up tight!"

He donned his armour, then he rode
to Pellinore's posh place.
And rude Sir P yelled, "Raspberry!"
And blew one in his face!

So then King Arthur and Sir P
set to, with *heys!* and *hoys!*
They clacked and clanged, they whacked
    and banged.
Good gracious! What a noise!

They fought like ferrets, fought like dogs,
they fought like crazy cats.
They had to hit each other hard
'cos both wore iron hats.

Now, Arthur gripped his shining sword
in both his metal mitts.
He clonked Sir P so mightily
the blade broke into bits.

Sir P was dizzy with the blow
but blinked and gave a grin.
He summoned up his henchmen,

It looked like Arthur's time was up.
His sword was just a stump.
Sir P's rough band with clubs in hand
were closing in to thump.

But then, across the battleground,
there flashed a blur of white.
Was it a wizard? Was it a whirlwind?
No! It was a knight!

"I come," he called, "upon my steed,
for King and Camelot.
To serve the Crown, I'll knock you down.
I am Sir Lancelot!"

His milk-white charger whirled around.
He whacked so many ways.
Kerlunk! Kerlang! Sir P's rough gang
lay sprawling in a daze.

Sir Pellinore cried, "Boo-hoo-hoo!
My helmet's got a dent.
My breastplate's burst, but what is worst -
my lovely lance is bent!"

"That's nothing," cried King Arthur.
"Your helmet's smashed my sword.
Another blade so nicely made
I simply can't afford."

But as he spoke there came a flash,
a flicker, then a fizz.
Before him stood old Merlin,
King Arthur's royal wiz.

He shook the sparkles from his cloak,
the fizzes from his hair,
then, as he spoke, began to poke
his finger in the air:

"As magic-maker to the court
I have things well in hand.
So come with me and soon you'll see
the sword that I have planned.

"It's being fashioned underground
with secret elvish skill.
With this fine sword you won't be bored.
You'll love it. Yes, you will.

"Sir Lancelot can go back home
to Camelot, for tea.
But, as for you, your sword awaits,
so come along with me."

King Arthur's eager face lit up.
"A brand new sword? That's great!
A magic sword made underground!
Wow! I can hardly wait!"

So Merlin and King Arthur
went riding off together.
They rode through mist, they rode
   through fog,
all kinds of spooky weather.

They seemed to ride forever
down weirdly winding trails,
while all around there came the sound
of strange and eerie wails.

They rode through deep, enchanted woods,
they rode through dreary bogs.
They heard the caw of ragged crows,
the howl of ghostly dogs.

Then Merlin took a little path
that ribboned round a hill,
and soon they came upon a lake
that lay completely still.

No birds sang in the silent trees.
No frogs went croak or hop.
No breezes whispered in the reeds.
No little fish went *plop!*

"But see," said Merlin, "yonder…
the centre of the lake…"
So Arthur looked, and at the sight
his legs began to shake.

A slender arm that gripped a sword
rose slowly from the water.
"I'll save her!" cried young Arthur.
"She must be some knight's daughter…"

"Be still," hissed Merlin. "There you see
the Lady of the Lake.
She's like a kind of mermaid.
That sword is yours to take."

The sword it shone so fine and true.
Its blade looked brave and trusty.
But Arthur thought,

Just then, beside him came a boat,
so Arthur climbed aboard.
It sailed as if by magic,
and took him to the sword.

He held the sword with trembling hands.
The boat slid back to shore.
Then both of them inspected it
And Arthur murmured,

Cor!

"With such a sword I'll challenge giants
and fierce foes to fights.
I'll take on brigands, really big 'uns,
also…nasty knights!"

"But let me tell you," Merlin said,
"that while the sword is ace,
it has a magic scabbard,
a strange, enchanted case.

"So thread the scabbard on your belt.
As long as it stays yours,
it works its charms against all harms -
yes, weapons, teeth and claws!"

With that, old Merlin vanished,
and Arthur scratched his head.
But then he saw some words upon
the handle, which he read:

I am Excalibur, your sword,
and I will never break.
But when your reign is over,
return me to the lake.

"Well, that will be a while, I hope,"
said Arthur, with a chuckle.
He put the scabbard on his belt
and fastened up the buckle.

He galloped back to Camelot
to show his knights the sword.
He held it high against the sky.
His knights all cheered and roared.

"A king with such a sword," they cried,
"is just the thing we need.
We'll all be loyal to you now
and follow where you lead.

"So take us off to fight with fiends
and other frightful foes.
We'll stop their nasty nonsense
and biff them on the nose."

Then young Arthur called a toast
with cups of fizzy wine:

To all who fight for what is right
and make things fair and fine!

My stirring tale is over now.
It's time for me to fly.
But stories more I have in store.
I'll tell them by and by.

Now, have you seen this trick before?
The one I use to go?
I flap my wings, say magic things,
and FEATHERS! I'm a crow!

CRAZY CAMELOT CAPERS

Written by Tony Mitton
Illustrated by Arthur Robins

Crazy Camelot Capers are available from all good bookshops,
or can be ordered direct from the publisher:
Orchard Books, PO BOX 29, Douglas IM99 1BQ
Credit card orders please telephone 01624 836000
or fax 01624 837033
or e-mail: bookshop@enterprise.net for details.

To order please quote title, author and ISBN
and your full name and address.
Cheques and postal orders should be
made payable to 'Bookpost plc'.
Postage and packing is FREE within the UK
(overseas customers should add £1.00 per book).

Prices and availability are subject to change.